OCT 0 5 2010

I REPEAT, DON'T CHEAT!

BY Margery Cuyler

ILLUSTRATED BY Arthur Howard

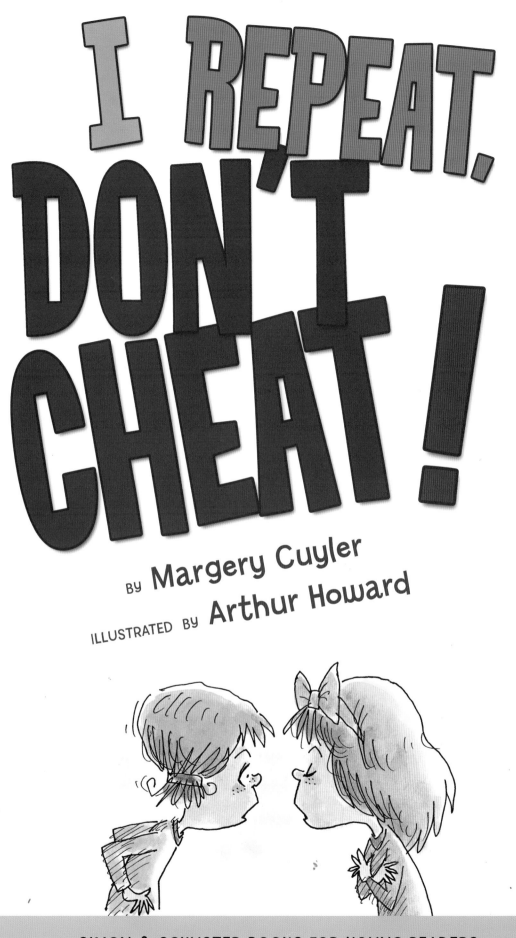

SIMON & SCHUSTER BOOKS FOR YOUNG READERS

New York   London   Toronto   Sydney

For Jul, with love—M. C.

SIMON & SCHUSTER BOOKS FOR YOUNG READERS
An imprint of Simon & Schuster Children's Publishing Division
1230 Avenue of the Americas, New York, New York 10020
Text copyright © 2010 by Margery Cuyler
Illustrations copyright © 2010 by Arthur Howard
For information about special discounts for bulk purchases, please contact Simon &
Schuster Special Sales at 1-866-506-1949 or business@simonandschuster.com.
The Simon & Schuster Speakers Bureau can bring authors to your live event. For more
information or to book an event, contact the Simon & Schuster Speakers Bureau at
1-866-248-3049 or visit our website at www.simonspeakers.com.

Book design by Laurent Linn
The text for this book is set in Billy.
The illustrations for this book are rendered in pen and ink with watercolor paints.
Manufactured in China
1109 SCP
2 4 6 8 10 9 7 5 3 1

Library of Congress Cataloging-in-Publication Data
Cuyler, Margery.
I repeat, don't cheat! / Margery Cuyler ; illustrated by Arthur Howard.—1st ed.
p. cm.
Summary: Jessica worries about the consequences of exposing a cheating friend.
ISBN 978-1-4169-7167-2 (hardcover)
[1. Cheating—Fiction. 2. Best friends—Fiction. 3. Friendship—Fiction.
4. Worry—Fiction. 5. Schools—Fiction.]
I. Howard, Arthur, ill. II. Title. III. Title: I repeat, do not cheat!
PZ7.C997Iak 2010
[E]—dc22
2009013955

JESSICA WAS A WORRYWART.

She worried about lots of things.

She worried about falling off her bike

and seeing aliens in the backyard

and getting bitten by a spider

and remembering to feed Wiggles.

But at school, Jessica had a new worry. Her best friend Lizzie.

Lizzie had started copying Jessica's spelling words when Mr. Martin gave a test.

Their teacher had explained *that* wasn't allowed.

"I repeat, don't cheat!" he had told the class.

Jessica wondered if she should tell
Mr. Martin.

But if she tattled on Lizzie, then
Lizzie wouldn't be her friend anymore.

So Jessica decided not to tell.

During recess Jessica had a *new* worry.
When she tagged Lizzie, Lizzie refused
to be *it*.

"You didn't tag me," she said.

"Did too!" yelled Jessica.

"Did not!" yelled Lizzie.

Jessica *knew* she had tagged her friend.

"I saw Jessica tag you too," said Sharad.
"You're *it*, Lizzie!"

"I don't want to play anymore," said Lizzie,
and she sat down on the grass.

Mrs. Hicks, the playground aide, came over.

"Are you all right?" she asked.

"Jessica says she tagged me," said Lizzie, "but she's lying."

"That's not true," said Sharad. "I saw her do it!"

"Are you sure you tagged Lizzie?" Mrs. Hicks asked Jessica.

Jessica was confused. If she told Mrs. Hicks
the truth, then Lizzie would be mad at her.

If Jessica didn't tell the truth, then *she*
would be lying.

Her worries felt like ants crawling in her
stomach.

"Maybe I thought I did, but I really didn't,"
she mumbled.

On Saturday Lizzie asked Jessica for a play date.

Jessica wasn't sure she wanted to go, but Lizzie said her mom would take them out for pizza.

So Jessica said yes.

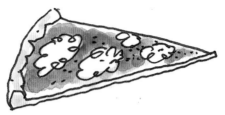

After pizza the two girls sat in Lizzie's room and drew pictures.

"You're really good at art," said Jessica.

"I like to draw," said Lizzie.

Lizzie went and got her workbook.

"Could you help me with my *T*-word poem?"
she asked.

Jessica decided this was okay. Mr. Martin
always let the kids help one another, except
during tests.

"You could write about a tree," said Jessica.

"That's boring," said Lizzie. "How about a tarantula?"

"Too hard to spell," said Jessica.

"How about a toe?" said Lizzie.

"Perfect," said Jessica. "What words describe a toe?"

"Warts," said Lizzie.

"Gross," said Jessica. "How about wiggly?"

"Okay," said Lizzie. "My toes are very wiggly."

"Anything else?" asked Jessica.

"Maybe later," said Lizzie, and she picked up a marker. "Let's draw some more."

"I can think of some other toe words," said Jessica.

So while Lizzie drew, Jessica finished the poem.

She wrote the words down in Lizzie's workbook.

toh

wigli
pink lik a ros
smal lik a nos
kurlee
soft

The next day Mr. Martin asked the class to share their poems.

Lizzie read Jessica's toe poem out loud.

"Great job!" said Mr. Martin.

Then he looked at Lizzie's workbook.

"And your writing looks nice and neat today too. I'm *very* happy with your progress."

Jessica knew she should be happy for
her friend too, but she felt miserable.

*That's really my poem that Mr. Martin
liked,* she thought, *but Lizzie didn't tell
him that I helped.*

Jessica wanted to say something, but
she wasn't sure she should.

So she sat in her chair and sulked.

When Mr. Martin asked Jessica to read *her* poem out loud, she wished she could disappear.

Her poem wasn't very good.

It was about a tree, and it was only two lines long.

"It's not finished," said Jessica.

But what she really wanted to say was, "Lizzie's already read my poem, the toe poem that you liked so much!"

That night Jessica couldn't sleep.

She tossed and turned.

Should she say something to Mr. Martin?

Should she say something to Lizzie?

Should she say something to Mom and Dad?

At breakfast Jessica didn't feel like eating.

She was too busy worrying about Lizzie.

"Do you feel all right?" asked Mom.

"Please pass the orange juice," said Tom.

"Where are my gym shorts?" said Laura.

"Where are my socks?" said Dad.

"Do best friends ever cheat?" asked Jessica.

"What?" said Mom.

Just then Jessica heard the bus outside.
She grabbed her lunch and math money
and ran out the door.

In class Mr. Martin asked the class to count their coins.

Lizzie whispered to Jessica, "Can you give me some of yours?"

This time Jessica didn't feel like helping Lizzie.

"No!" she said. "You'll have to borrow from someone else."

Quickly Lizzie stuck her hand into Jessica's money jar.

"Stop that!" shouted Jessica.

Mr. Martin rushed over.

"What's the trouble?" he asked.

"Lizzie took some of my money," said Jessica. "And that poem about the toe is *my* poem, not Lizzie's."

Lizzie's face turned as red as a geranium.

"Lizzie," said Mr. Martin, "did you take Jessica's money without asking?"

"No," said Lizzie, "I mean, yes, I did. Because Jessica wouldn't share."

"But if you had asked nicely," said Mr. Martin, "I'm sure she *would* have shared."

"I did ask nicely," said Lizzie, "but she just got mad."

Jessica couldn't believe her ears.

Now she was *really* mad.

Words gushed out of her like lava.

"Lizzie asked me to help her with her poem, but *I* ended up writing the whole thing," she blurted, "and she copied my spelling words and—"

"That's enough," interrupted Mr. Martin. "It looks as if Lizzie has made some poor choices. Lizzie, I think you need to sit at the thinking desk until you sort things out.

"And, Jessica, it was nice of you to help your friend, but there's a difference between *helping* and *doing*."

Jessica sighed. She looked down at her own poem.

Then she wrote:

Tal like a giraf
   ponty lik a pensel.
leevs
clap
in the win.

She drew a tree above the words.

It wasn't as nice a tree as Lizzie would have drawn, but it was good enough.

"Great job!" said Mr. Martin,
and he tacked Jessica's work on
the bulletin board.

The next day Lizzie told Mr. Martin, "I don't need to sit at the thinking desk anymore. I'm going to do my own work from now on."

Lizzie walked over to Jessica. "I'm sorry for all the things I did that made you mad. I made you a present."

Lizzie had drawn a picture of her and Jessica.
Scribbled on top were the words:

Jessica gave Lizzie a hug.

"You're still my best friend," she

said. "And you're a great artist!"

"You're still my best friend too,"

said Lizzie. "And you're a great poet!"

BEST FRIENDS FOREVER!